W9-ATT-210

Dedicated to my family

Published 1992 by Thomasson-Grant, Inc. All rights reserved.
Text and photographs on pages 4, 12, and 15 © 1992 Elizabeth Henning Sutton.
Photographs on cover and pages 1, 8, 11, 16, 21, 22, 25, 27, 28, 31, 32, 35, 37, 38, 41, 43, 45, and
46 © Robert Llewellyn.

99 98 97 96 95 94 93 92   5 4 3 2 1

Library of Congress Cataloging-in-Publication Data

Sutton, Elizabeth Henning.
     The pony champions / Elizabeth Henning Sutton.
         p.   cm.
     Summary: Careless and rushed in her attempt to juggle her time between preparing for a
pony competition and a tap dance recital, busy fourth grader Meg allows her pony Lady Jane
to become very sick.
     ISBN 1-56566-019-6
     [1. Ponies—Fiction.]   I. Title.
PZ7.S96815Pn   1992
[Fic]—dc20   92-10518
                                                                      CIP
                                                                       AC

Thomasson-Grant
One Morton Drive
Charlottesville, Virginia 22901
(804) 977-1780

THE PONY CHAMPIONS

Elizabeth Henning Sutton

THOMASSON-GRANT
Charlottesville, Virginia

CHAPTER I

Friday

Early one bright spring morning the Jackson family was sound asleep. Tommy and David snuggled deep in their warm covers. The alarm clock buzzed like an angry bee in Mother and Father's room. Meg heard it all the way down the hall. She opened her eyes, climbed out of bed, and looked out her window at the sun-drenched lawn glistening with dew. Nearby in a dogwood tree, a happy goldfinch sang. Meg took a deep breath. She loved the smell of grass after a rain.

Thank goodness the sun finally came out! she thought. That means this afternoon we can—

"Get up, Meg!" called her father. "David, Tommy, you'll be late for school." In the room next door, the two boys yawned and rubbed the sleep from their eyes.

"What is the weather going to be like?" asked Tommy, who was nine. "What should we wear?"

"It's sunny and warm. Wear jeans," answered Mother, who was on her way downstairs. Meg was the first one to the table, her backpack zipped and her hair combed.

"My, aren't we perky today!" said Mother.

"Today is Friday! We're going riding after school, right?"

"Unless it rains."

"The show is on Sunday, and we *have* to ride today. We missed a lot last week, and we have to practice for the horse show."

"We'll see how well you do today and tomorrow before we decide whether or not you're ready to ride in the show. Besides, you and David have your work cut out for you with two white ponies to groom and all this mud."

5

Mother packed the children's lunches as they finished their breakfast. Tommy grabbed his lunch and pulled his book bag over his shoulder. He and Meg left for school together, walking to the end of their lane to meet the bus. David was lucky. He was in the sixth grade, and the middle school bus did not come so early.

Meg was a very busy fourth grader. As she walked along with her brother, she thought about all of her responsibilities. There were her pets—Marshmallow, the rabbit, and Buck, the dog, who had to be fed every day. Not to mention the homework assignments her teacher piled on. She also managed to take tap dancing lessons once a week. But of all her activities, her favorite was riding her own pony, Lady Jane. Riding was her best sport, and her pony was her best friend.

Every Friday afternoon Mother took Meg and David out into the country to the farm where they boarded their horses. Tommy went to Little League baseball practice, for even though he loved horses, he wasn't interested in riding them. He much preferred the excitement of any sport that had a ball to throw, kick, hit, or catch. He couldn't wait to hit his first home run. But Meg and David had been taking riding lessons since they were seven, and they loved it, especially when the two of them went riding with their mother and her horse, Another.

"Mom," asked Meg as they drove along, "I know you've told me before, but how did Another get his name? Why didn't they call him Big Boy or something normal like that?"

"His former owner had so many horses to take care of that when he was born she said, 'I cannot keep another.' So her daughter decided to name the little colt Another. Later, they gave him away to a trainer. We bought him when he was four, and we kept the name."

"Blue has papers, doesn't he?" asked David.

"Yes, he is a purebred registered Welsh Mountain pony. Unlike Another's name, Blue's name tells us about his parents, a famous stallion named Fiddling Blue Danube, and a fine mare named Dixie Darling. His full name is Dixie Blue Devil.

Meg had never thought about it before, but the name Lady Jane seemed just right for the pretty pony waiting to greet her as they arrived at the stable. Janie whinnied with delight as she saw Meg coming to let her out of her paddock.

Another pushed in front of David's pony, Blue, and pawed at the ground, begging to be let out as well. In turn, each animal was led to the stable to get ready for the ride. First, they had to be groomed. Moses, a large, lazy tabby cat, was disturbed from his nap atop the saddle pad on the tack trunk when Meg moved her grooming kit.

"You must have chased a lot of mice last night," said Meg as she stroked his back. He rolled over and purred, barely opening one eye.

"Oh, Janie!" complained Meg as she scrubbed the loose hair and caked mud from the pony's coat. "How did you ever get so muddy? You look like a bowl of vanilla ice cream covered with hard sauce!"

"What a pig!" said David. "Blue is filthy." His currycomb sent a cloud of red dust into the air.

Mother sneezed. "Another, you're as bad as those ponies." She brushed away the dirt and stains that covered the big horse's grey coat. "I sure am glad you're not going to the pony show Sunday. I'd never get you clean!" This was just fine with Another. He did not mind being brown, and the mud felt good when he rolled in it. Baths were usually a nuisance, unless of course it was a hot summer day. Then the hose felt cool and refreshing.

Meg cleaned Janie's hooves with a hoof pick, then carefully combed the tangles from her mane. She spread a clean saddle pad on the pony's back before gently placing the saddle on the withers. She noticed how easy it was to tack up, now that she was much taller. When she first got Lady Jane three years ago, it took her forever, and she always needed Mother to help.

"Hurry, slow poke!" called David, who had already mounted Blue.
"What are you doing in there?"

"Don't forget to tighten the girth. You know how ponies love to puff
themselves up," Mother said as she led Another outside.

Meg arched her back as she inched the girth a hole tighter. Lady Jane
did not like having her girth too tight, so Meg was careful to be gentle.
Meg grabbed her crop and helmet and went to join her family. She climbed
easily into the saddle and rode to catch up before they left her behind.

It was a beautiful day, but the ring was too wet to practice jumping, so
they decided to take a trail ride. There was a path through the woods that
led to a grassy field alongside the river. It was David's favorite place to
gallop Blue, for it seemed to go on forever. As soon as they got there,
Another and Blue moved faster, but Lady Jane's little legs could not keep
up.

"Wait!" Meg yelled. Mother and Another heard her and stopped to wait. Another loved the two ponies and did not want to go on without them, since he was accustomed to leading them on the trail. He did not like Lady Jane to be out of his sight.

"Please don't go so fast," pleaded Meg when she caught up with Mother.

"We're not going fast. You're just going too slowly. That pony is too small to keep up with us," said David.

"She is NOT!" insisted Meg.

"Let's trot over to those big rocks," said Mother in an effort to change the subject and avoid an argument. "Last one there is a rotten egg!" And with that, the two children raced across the field. Since Meg was closest to the ground, she was off Lady Jane in an instant, with David close behind her. They tossed their reins to Mother to hold for them and crawled up the boulder like two little lizards on a garden wall. "I beat you!" Meg said proudly when she reached the top.

Meg loved the feeling of freedom that riding in the country gave her. She loved playing games with David, and it was fun taking the ponies on picnics to Grandma's farm. But lately, Meg had begun to think about what would happen to Lady Jane when she got too big to ride her. She could not bear the idea of selling her, but she knew that she couldn't ride her forever. She also knew that her parents could not afford to keep a pony too little for anyone in the family to ride. Who could ever love her or take care of her as well as Meg did?

"Let's go now," said Mother as she turned Another's head toward home. With a quick step, the ponies followed right behind.

Back at the barn, Mother and the children put away their tack and rubbed the sweat marks from Another and the ponies. They checked their stalls, where Judy, the stable manager, had given each one fresh water and hay. In the feed room Mother was measuring out the portions of grain for Another and Blue. Lady Jane strained at her lead rope to get a mouthful.

"Why can't we feed Janie oats like the other horses? She is hungry," complained Meg.

"She has plenty of hay to eat. Remember, she has foundered."

Meg thought about the time last spring. Janie's feet were so sore she could hardly walk after she spent a week in the big pasture with the rest of the mares.

"That's why we keep her off grass in the spring. You have to be careful with ponies. If they get into grain, they won't stop eating the way a horse will. Janie would eat herself to death if we let her. She can only have a handful."

Meg remembered the time Blue got colic from eating moldy hay. He kicked at his sides, lay down, and rolled in his stall. He was so uncomfortable. David had to make him get up and walk, to keep him from getting a twisted intestine.

"Well, I guess these can't hurt you," said Meg as she fed the pony two sugar cubes. Lady Jane crunched them happily and nudged Meg, looking for more.

"That's all, pretty girl. I'll see you tomorrow." Meg fastened the latch on the gate, then snapped the extra chain to double lock it. She knew her pony was an escape artist, and she wasn't taking any chances. Lady Jane knew how to wiggle the gate with her nose to loosen the gate hook, and once before, she had gotten out. Luckily, Meg caught her and was careful to snap the chain after that.

"Remember to lock—" began David.

"I know, the feed room," called Meg as she walked toward the barn. She pulled the door with a firm tug, heard the lock click, and turned out the lights.

CHAPTER II

Saturday Morning

Meg had just finished cleaning up her room when she suddenly remembered. "Oh, no!" she gasped.

"What?" asked Mother.

"Today is the dress rehearsal for our tap recital next week!"

"That's okay."

"No, it isn't! How can I ride and get Janie ready for the show tomorrow and go to the theater too?"

"Well," said Mother thoughtfully, "couldn't you skip this show and just wait until the one next month? There are lots of shows coming up, but this is your only recital."

"I *have* to ride Sunday. Aunt Liz and Anna are coming all the way from Washington to see us."

"It'll be a big rush for you to practice both dance and riding this afternoon. We're going to the barn at one o'clock, and your rehearsal's at 12:30," Mother said. She thought for a moment. "I suppose if your father could drive you to the stable after the rehearsal and Tommy's Little League—"

"That's an idea!"

"You'd just have time to ride late this afternoon. Tomorrow morning you'll have to bathe Janie and clean your tack at seven before the show. The choice is yours. I still think it would be better to concentrate on one thing at a time."

Meg knew how important it was for her and her pony to be well prepared. She and Lady Jane had won the Short Stirrup championship last summer, and she had not forgotten the thrill she felt when she heard their names called over the loudspeaker: "LADY JANE GREY, RIDDEN BY MEG

JACKSON. CHAMPION!" She treasured the silver trophy and the beautiful flowing ribbon. Mother and Father had framed the picture they took of her and Lady Jane that day. It hung on her bedroom wall, and she felt proud whenever she saw it. She just knew she could win again, as long as she did her best.

This year all her friends were taking tap dancing. Mondays after school Meg went with them to practice the many steps that went into making a dance routine. She loved the clicking sounds her special shoes made and the wonderful sequined costumes that sparkled under the stage lights. She loved the music, the excitement, and the applause almost as much as she loved the way she felt when she was in a horse show.

"Meg, what do you want to do?" asked Father.

"I want to dance," said Meg, "and I think I can ride too, if you'll help get me there." Besides, she thought, I may not be able to show Janie much longer. Meg had grown a couple of inches since last summer. This show was important. She wanted to go, no matter what.

Meg decided to get her clothes ready to save time later. There was a lot to do. First, she packed a duffle bag with all of her dance things. There was a satin and tulle skirt, a leotard covered in delicate sequins and ribbons, a headpiece, a hat, and of course the patent leather pumps with silver metal on the toes and heels. With some lipstick and rouge, hairpins and spray, and her best hairbrush, the bag was ready.

For her trip to the barn that afternoon, she put some jeans, a T-shirt, and her boots into her backpack. She would change at the stable. For tomorrow's show, she collected all the clothes she would need and folded them neatly over the chair in her room: jodhpurs, a ratcatcher shirt, a dark blue jacket, leather knee straps, elastic clips to hold her pants down over her boots, gloves, and a hairnet.

David was already polishing his boots. Meg picked up a rag and set to work on her own, which were covered with a week's worth of dirt.

14

"Sometimes I wonder why we do all this work," grumbled David. "I like to show and all, but tennis and baseball are a lot easier. All you have to do is get dressed and play."

"Tennis balls aren't happy to see you when you get to the game, and a baseball bat doesn't think for you when you forget the play," Meg replied.

"I know," he sighed. David rubbed his boots until he could see them shine. Somehow he felt proud that no one would look at him tomorrow and ask, "Who is that sloppy-looking kid?" He imagined how great his pony would be. He knew that in a horse show your appearance had to be as outstanding as your performance.

CHAPTER III

Practice, Practice, Practice

On their way to Meg's rehearsal, she and David sat quietly in the back seat. David was anxious to ride Blue, who had missed his usual exercise that week because of the rain. He needed to warm up in the ring and then practice every jump that they would be making tomorrow. Every part of their ride had to be planned so that it would look smooth and easy to the judge. Every fence had to be perfect, and Blue had to move well enough to beat good ponies like Rocket Rhythm, who was a consistent winner.

David secretly wished that Rocket and her owner, Mary Keith, would get sick or that Mary would change her mind about going to the show tomorrow. He had seen her at school on Friday, and she had said that she would see him there. "I don't see why they even bother to come to our stable. Don't they usually go for points in big recognized shows anyway?" David said aloud. "Mary was the high-score equitation champion at the state fair last summer. She'll probably cream us!"

"Don't forget," Mother chimed in, "Rocket's not the only great pony in the neighborhood. If I'm not mistaken, Mary won that equitation class on an older pony. Rocket Rhythm is very talented, but she's still a little green. Mary hasn't shown her much since they bought her. She is probably using this local show for practice."

"Yeah," said Meg. "I heard they paid more for that pony than Dad spent on his new car! I bet she even has a groom to do all the work for her. What a princess!"

"Meg!" scolded Mother. "It is not nice to discuss what other people may or may not pay for their belongings. Do you ever think of money and what our ponies are worth to us?"

"If we had to put a dollar value on Lady Jane, or Another, or Blue, what would it be?" David asked.

"About two million," said Meg, who did not like to think about selling ponies. She sighed, feeling thankful that Mary Keith would not be riding in her division the next day. For the moment, Meg had a stage show to think about.

She went over all the steps in her mind so that she could dance in the rehearsal without forgetting anything. She knew that the two minutes they were on stage included a hundred tiny movements. If those hundred movements were done well, the audience only saw one movement: twelve dancers performing in unison.

"Riding in a show is a little like a recital," she said to her mother, "except you and the pony are the dancers, and you have to dance better than everyone else to make the judge notice you!" It was a challenge. Meg wanted to ride well so that Lady Jane would look her very best.

The rehearsal was over before Meg knew it. The girls looked like a real chorus line as they flawlessly went through their dance. Meg loved the stage flooded with light, and the deafening clatter of the tap shoes. She couldn't wait for the real show to begin next Saturday. She left the theater, calling goodbyes to her friends, as Father waited to pick her up at the curb. Tommy was sitting in the back seat, munching peanuts.

"How was baseball?" asked Meg, immediately noticing his grimy uniform and sitting a safe distance away. "What did you do, clean the bat with your bare hands?" Tommy reached toward his sister with a mud-covered fist.

"Here," he said. "Give these to Lady Jane for me, okay?"

"What?" exclaimed Meg. He handed her a handful of peppermints he had been saving in his jacket pocket for his next visit to the stable. "Thanks a lot!" she said. It is funny, thought Meg, how brothers can act sweeter than they look sometimes.

According to plan, they went directly to the stable, where Mother and

18

David were just getting ready to clean their tack. David and Blue were finished with their rehearsal, and Lady Jane waited patiently for hers to begin.

"I'm sorry I'm late!" said Meg as she rushed past her brother.

She brought her pony inside and began to get ready to ride. Since she was in a hurry, she didn't bother with grooming and put the saddle on Janie's back with a thump. When Meg reached under her belly and tightened the girth with a sharp tug, Lady Jane pinned back her ears and gave a hurt look. Meg usually was more gentle.

"I'm sorry," said Meg. "I forgot you hate that." Lady Jane switched her tail as if to say, "Don't do it again."

Meg put the bridle on more carefully and snapped her helmet in place. In a moment they were in the ring, going over all the transitions and movements at walk, trot, and canter that they would have to do well the next day. At the trot, she practiced her diagonals, moving up and down in harmony with the rise and fall of her pony's outside shoulder. To make a smooth change from a trot to a canter, Janie had to obey the cue from Meg's squeeze of the leg and lead with her inside hoof. An incorrect lead or wrong diagonal would cost Meg valuable points. She knew she had to get it right the first time, for in a show there were no second chances.

For reasons that Meg did not understand, Lady Jane did not cooperate as she usually did. When Meg asked her to canter, she bucked. She laid back her ears when they trotted. Things became worse when they tried to jump. Instead of trotting smoothly over the fence, Janie ran around it. Meg was upset and worried about the show. Lady Jane could sense her rider's feelings through the tightly held reins and the awkward kicks of her legs.

"What is wrong with her?" Meg cried. Her mother was watching from the gate. She could see that Meg was in a hurry to finish and catch up with her brother, who was ready to go home. As she had feared, it seemed as if

Meg was running out of patience and energy after such a long day.

"Slow everything down. You're rushing her." Mother could see how Meg's irritable temper was affecting her pony's performance.

"She never acts like this!"

"She's probably in a cranky mood," said Mother. "Be patient with her."

But Meg was feeling cranky too. She was in no mood to ride well, and she did not want to keep everyone so late the night before the show. David would probably call her a slow poke, or say something mean about how her pony behaved. She decided to quit for the day. The more she rode, the more unhappy Lady Jane seemed to become. Maybe things would be better in the morning.

Meg took off her tack and put it on the floor by the door to take home. She would clean it later. She put on Janie's halter and put the bridle over her saddle on the floor. She left Janie tied while she went into the feed room to get the pony something to eat. She forgot all about Tommy's peppermints in the grooming kit where she left them. With a bucket in one hand and the lead rope in the other, she led Lady Jane out to her little paddock. Mother was in the car with the motor running, and David was watching her from the front seat. Meg pulled the gate closed and picked up her saddle and bridle on the way to the car. As they drove away, she did not see that the light in the feed room was shining through the open door. The chain on Janie's gate was hanging loose, unsnapped.

CHAPTER IV

Emergency in the Night

It was a moonless night. The clock beside Mother's bed said 3:34. The phone rang twice before she snatched it off the hook.

"Hello?" she mumbled sleepily. Then suddenly she was wide awake.

"When?" she asked. "Have you called the vet?" Mother listened carefully to the voice at the end of the line. She sat upright in bed.

"Good, Judy. Thanks so much for calling. Please keep her moving until we get there. It'll be fifteen minutes." Mother went straight to Meg's room to wake her.

"Get out of bed, honey." Meg rolled away from her. Mother gently shook her shoulder and said, "Meg, it's Janie. She is very sick and we have to go to the stable NOW!"

As she drove through the night to the stable, Mother told Meg what had happened.

"Somebody forgot to lock the feed room door last night, and Lady Jane got out. They found her in the barn an hour ago, licking up what was left of several bags of feed on the floor." Meg felt a queasy pain in her stomach. No one had to tell her what this meant. She could hardly stand the thought of what she had done. It was all her fault.

The barn was lit from one end to the other when they arrived Judy was leading the little pony up and down the aisle. Open sacks of feed were scattered outside the feed room door. Another was the only other horse in the stable. The rest were out as usual.

"I tried to put her in a stall while I cleaned up this mess, but after a few minutes she started acting really strange—kicking her stomach and trying to roll," said Judy.

"Why is Another here?" asked Meg as she took the lead rope.

23

"If it weren't for him, I wouldn't have known something was wrong. He must have seen that she was loose, and he almost ran himself lame whinnying up and down the fence. You know how he can't stand it if one of those ponies goes out without him!"

Meg stroked Janie's forehead. The little pony's eyes rolled with fright, searching everyone's face for a solution to her torment. She was restless. She pushed Meg roughly with her nose. She would stand, quivering for a moment, then begin to turn and stamp her feet. The muscles of her belly were tight, and her nostrils flared with heavy breathing.

"Poor, poor Lady Jane! I'm so sorry," cried Meg.

"She must have eaten more feed than I like to imagine," said Judy. "I found her in there with her whole body practically in the bin. It's a wonder she hasn't burst!"

Meg was crying. Mother was just off the phone with the vet's answering service.

"Dr. Foley will be here in a few minutes. Hang on. She'll be okay," said Mother hopefully. "Try to keep her walking."

Lady Jane did not want to walk. Her stomach was one big spasm of pain. Down she dropped to her knees onto the ground outside the stable. She began to roll, grunting and groaning. Mother took the rope from Meg and yanked hard at the pony's head. She spoke to Lady Jane in a tone that meant business. "You *are* getting up, Janie. Come on, girl!"

Meg wished that she was the one who was sick instead of her little pony, who couldn't tell anyone how bad she felt. It was horrible seeing her suffer.

How could she be so stupid? How many times had she been warned to check the gate and lock the door? A few hours ago she was dreaming of a championship, and now she was living a nightmare! Janie's life *depended* on her. She had let her down. If anything happened to her pony, she had only herself to blame.

The minute the vet arrived, he hurried to the pony's side. He ran a hand over her flanks and leaned down to listen with his stethoscope.

"No bowel sounds at all," he said. His face was grim. "That means an impaction. Has she been trying to lie down?" he asked. After they explained what had happened, he went to work to relieve her discomfort. He took a large syringe and stuck the needle into Janie's neck. Meg felt weak. It was the biggest shot she had ever seen.

"That will make her relax and feel better fast," explained the doctor. Next, he took a plastic tube out of a bucket of warm water, and pushed it down her nostril into the little pony's stomach. Meg covered her eyes. Lady Jane made a coughing sound.

"It doesn't hurt, honey," Mother reassured her. "It just looks painful."

"This mineral oil I'm putting down her will help all the feed go through quickly. Otherwise, she could not digest it, and that would be very dangerous. We need to get it moving out of there."

"Is she going to die?" cried Meg. She put her arms gently around the little pony's neck. Lady Jane was breathing in a short, quick rhythm. "Please don't die, Janie! You have to get better, please! We love you too much!"

"Meg," said the doctor, "she is very, very sick. With the amount of food she has eaten, there is danger of a rupture or a twisted intestine. You found her just in time. If we watch her for the next few hours and keep her calm, the feed will probably move through her and she'll feel better soon. Don't let her roll, and make her walk if she gets restless."

The doctor put his equipment back in the big truck while Meg led her pony to a comfortable stall.

"Nothing to eat. NOTHING. For twenty four hours, okay?" he said looking sternly at Judy, Mother, and Meg. "Call me if you have any problems at all; I'll be on duty all day."

Mother put her arms around Meg as they watched the vet drive away. Meg was thinking about how close she had just come to losing her pony. She had tried to do too many things that afternoon, and being in a hurry had nearly cost Lady Jane her life. She prayed that Lady Jane would safely make it through the rest of the night. The dawn sky was barely turning pink above the mountains that surrounded the farm. A new day was beginning.

CHAPTER V

Sunday Morning—Showtime!

David and Father were waiting when Mother arrived home a little after five that morning. The kitchen smelled of coffee and hot cocoa.

"How is she?" they asked.

"She'll probably be all right, but we won't know for sure for a while."

"Where's Meg?" asked Father.

"Still at the stable. She wanted to stay near the pony." Knowing how big brothers could be sometimes, Mother warned David, "She feels responsible for the pony's getting out, so don't *you* say a word. She feels bad enough as it is."

In just a couple of hours it would be time to get Blue and David ready for the show.

"Go on and get some sleep, David. You have a big day ahead of you," said Mother.

David thought about how scared he would be if the vet said Blue might not get better. He had seen colic once, and he would never forget it. Meg will never get over it if anything happens to that pony, he thought. She will think she did it.

"Go on now. I'll call you at seven," Mother said.

When they returned to the stable three hours later, Lady Jane was standing quietly in the corner of the stall. Meg was curled up on a clean horse blanket, and Moses was weaving in and out underneath her chin, purring loudly.

"Rise and shine!" said David. "It's showtime!"

Meg gave her brother a withering look.

"Speak for yourself!" she replied.

"What's wrong with you?" David asked.

"What's wrong? You don't know what's wrong? Didn't anyone tell you?"

"I know Janie had colic last night," David explained, "but she seems much better to me." He stroked Janie's neck.

"I see she has made a nice mess for us to clean up, and that's a good sign!" said Mother. "Has she been quiet since Dr. Foley left?"

"She has been standing right here, half asleep."

"If Janie is sick, Meg, that doesn't mean you can't ride," said David.

"Ride? Are you crazy? The vet said—"

"You moron, you can ride *another* pony in the show."

"Sure. Like who's going to lend me a pony the day of the show?"

"Like maybe me, that's who."

Meg was sure she was dreaming. Either David had totally lost his mind, or she had heard him wrong. Her brother never let anyone else ride his pony. She had only sat on Blue once or twice.

"I figured Blue could be entered in the Pony Hunter division with two riders," said David.

"And us riding double?" asked Meg.

"Boy, you still don't get it. *You* could take him in the Under Saddle class for the walk, trot, and canter, and *I* would ride in the two Over Fences classes. We'd share the division. The pony gets the ribbons, remember? It's different from Short Stirrup."

Mother overheard the conversation. "You can do it, honey. I know you can," she said gently. "We can all take turns coming down here to check on Lady Jane." She reminded Meg that their favorite aunt and little cousin Anna were on their way to see them ride in the show today. Anna loved to help with Lady Jane.

"You won't get many offers like this one," said her brother. "Besides, you're almost too old for Short Stirrup anyway. This will be good practice."

"But I've never even tried Blue! What if I forget to do something, or make a mistake?"

"Trust Blue. He knows what to do in a hack class. We've done this together a million times. It is just the same as riding Lady Jane. You'll just be a little higher off the ground, that's all."

Mother handed Meg a tote bag neatly packed with all of her show clothes. "They were all laid out on your chair. Put them on, and let's get going!"

CHAPTER VI

The Pony Hunters

By the time the announcer called for all entries in the Pony Hunter division, one very clean white pony and his two well-turned-out riders were waiting at the in gate.

"PONY HUNTER UNDER SADDLE, CLASS 10, ENTER THE RING AT THIS TIME, PLEASE."

"I feel sick," said Meg. Her face was flushed.

"You look great!" said Father.

"Just sit up straight and give yourself room. Blue will be fine," said David.

"Smile!" Mother whispered as Meg rode into the ring. In a few minutes, the judging began.

"TROT, PLEASE."

It took a moment for Meg to respond, but Blue trotted anyway. The next thing she knew, Meg was too close behind the pony in front of her. He is running away! she thought. What do I do? What did David say? Give myself room?

She saw a clear spot on the rail up ahead and headed across the ring straight for it. As she guided Blue back into line in front of a golden chestnut pony, she looked up and stared directly into the smiling eyes of Mary Keith. My goodness, she thought. How will the judge ever notice us with Rocket Rhythm right behind me? Rocket's coat was sleek and shiny, with reddish highlights that sparkled in the sunlight. Her mane was neatly braided all the way down her neck. Mary's hands guided each movement as she rode to Rocket's gently swinging walk in regal comfort. They looked brilliant together. Rocket moved along so smoothly that her feet hardly seemed to touch the ground.

Meg looked down at Blue's neck and noticed that each of his braids was a little different. Getting him ready that morning had been a group effort, and his lumpy mane showed it. Now, it was too late to worry about little things like braids.

It was amazing how much bigger Blue felt than her own little pony, whose two steps made one of his. Meg concentrated on getting her diagonals correct and preparing for what she knew would be the next command.

By the time the announcer said, "CANTER, PLEASE," Meg relaxed and rode Blue instead of sitting there as a passenger. It felt wonderful as he rocked along, smoothly covering ground. She smiled at her family, who watched her from the side of the ring.

"LINE UP AND FACE THE RINGMASTER, PLEASE!"

Thirteen ponies lined up for the judge to call the winning numbers. Meg's heart was pounding. She closed her eyes.

"IN FIRST PLACE, ROCKET RHYTHM, OWNED AND RIDDEN BY—"

Meg's heart sank, although she wasn't surprised. After all, she was there for the experience. And there was no doubt—Rocket was almost perfect. The announcer called two more numbers. Then:

"FOURTH PLACE, DIXIE BLUE DEVIL, OWNED BY DAVID JACKSON, RIDDEN BY MEG JACKSON."

Could she have heard it right? A little blonde Short Stirrup contestant handed her a white ribbon, which she gave to Mother as she rode triumphantly out of the gate. Her heart was bursting with pride.

"Meg, you were terrific!" said Mother.

"Not bad for a beginner!" teased David as they readjusted the stirrup leathers for his longer legs. Meg happily gave the reins to her brother, who led Blue to a shady spot under a tree. "That's a good boy, my Blue." David stroked Blue's neck and smiled. Meg was suddenly weak and very tired. Her mouth was terribly dry. It was over, and now it was David's turn.

"Where is Lady Jane?" asked a little voice coming up behind her.

"Why aren't you riding her?"

Meg looked and saw her cousin. "Anna!" she shrieked, giving the little six-year-old a big hug.

"When did you get here?" asked Meg. She explained to her cousin about Lady Jane and the feed bin.

"That's so sad!" Anna said. "How is she?"

"She is still not feeling well. We'll go check on her in just a little while. Do you want to see David and Blue? They're going in soon—this is their class."

David was already carefully watching Rocket Rhythm as she made her way around the course of eight jumps. Over and over, David repeated the order in which he had to take each fence. "Vertical, picket, inside diagonal to the wall—" Rocket was doing well until, all of a sudden, she refused to jump the wall and ran out to the left. Mary gave her a swift kick and circled back to try the jump again. The pony eyed the jump, flared her

nostrils, and planted her feet. As Mary smacked her with a loud thwack of the crop, she bolted from a standstill, swerving to the side once more and throwing Mary up over her neck and onto the ground on the other side of the wall. Fortunately, Mary was all right. She stood up and brushed herself off.

David watched in surprise and fear. What if Blue tried that with him? This was Rocket, a champion pony!

"THANK YOU!" The announcer signaled the contestant to leave the ring. Next, it was Blue's turn.

"NOW ON COURSE, NUMBER 301, DIXIE BLUE DEVIL."

"Come on, boy," David whispered as they approached the red-and-white poles.

All sound seemed to cease as the pair continued from one fence to the next. Mother kept her fingers crossed, then exhaled with relief. "He got the change," she whispered to Meg, who watched in admiration as David gave Blue an invisible signal to switch leads smoothly in midstride before he balanced himself for the turn. Blue cantered on in a flowing, steady pace. Every jump seemed to fall before him just right, and he jumped with ease. Down they came, across the diagonal towards the final jump—the brush.

"Moses!" gasped Mother. A brown-and-white shape scampered out from underneath the evergreen branches and shot like a bullet out of the ring.

"A CAT!" squealed Anna, pointing her finger. For a split second, Blue slowed his pace, distracted by the furry blur out of the corner of his eye. Instinctively, David pressed on, clucking to his pony with a reassuring squeeze as they took flight over the jump. David could feel that the ride was not perfect. But he was relieved to have finished the course. Blue gave a big snort as he walked toward the gate.

"Good job!" said Father.

"Good riding!" said Mother.

"Did you see Moses? Boy, you were lucky he didn't spook Blue!" added Meg.

David wanted to ride his second and last course as soon as he could. He and Blue were ready to try again. It seemed as though they would wait forever. He dismounted and removed his helmet.

"THE RESULTS OF CLASS 11, PONY HUNTER OVER FENCES. PLEASE JOG YOUR PONIES INTO THE RING IN THIS ORDER: 490, 301, 145, 140—"

"Second—wow!" said Tommy. He had not been watching his brother, and now he wished he had. After about five ponies jumped the same jumps over and over, Tommy had trouble paying attention. But he liked to watch when it was someone important, like his brother or sister. Meg and Mother and Father were all smiling and happy as they passed around the red ribbon.

"If we can win the next class—" David began.

"So long as you have fun and do the best you can, that is all that matters," declared Father.

"I know, I know," said David. "But winning is more fun than losing!"

CHAPTER VII

Meg's Moment

"NUMBER 301, ON DECK!"

David's turn had finally arrived. He walked Blue back and forth in front of the gate. They were ready to get on course and end the waiting.

"Go in there and have a good time!" said Mother. "This is fun, remember?"

David's helmet was damp with perspiration. His gloves were stuck to his hands. He went over the course in his mind once more before he was called. Then all eyes followed Blue into the ring. That is, except for Tommy and Anna, who scurried off to look for Moses.

This time as they rounded the turn to the first jump, the troublesome brush loomed ahead. David rode right to it with a firm leg and a steady hand. Next, they sailed over the picket fence and smoothly turned toward the next line of jumps. David blinked the moisture from his eyes. The rest of the course came fast, and before he knew it, cheers and whistles told him that they had finished in fine form. Meg was cheering the loudest.

"I rode every jump with you that time! You both were great, really good," she said.

David patted his pony and loosened the girth. He was ready to go back to the stable and cool off. Mother brushed the dirt from beneath Blue's belly and smoothed his mane.

"You'd better not leave just yet," she said. "They'll announce the results in a minute." David waited, watching the final rounds of the other riders, except for Mary, who had completed her last fence while he was discussing his performance with Mother and Meg. He wondered if he had done as well as they had.

Finally, the class was complete. The minutes passed slowly as the judge made his decisions final.

"WOULD THE FOLLOWING RIDERS JOG YOUR PONIES IN THIS ORDER: 301, 685—"

"We won!" cried David. Meg patted Blue as he went past her into the ring.

"That is amazing. He did it! And to come in first, ahead of Rocket—she's a super pony!" David was smiling from ear to ear as he pulled off his coat and took off his tie, handing the blue ribbon to Mother.

"THERE IS A TIE FOR CHAMPION IN THIS DIVISION: 301, DIXIE BLUE DEVIL, *AND* 685, ROCKET RHYTHM. PLEASE RETURN TO THE RING FOR A HACK OFF."

"What?" exclaimed David. "We only got a fourth in the Under Saddle, and Rocket was disqualified in one of the jumping classes!"

"It doesn't matter—your points are the same because she won the Under Saddle class," said Mother.

"Hurry! Get in the ring, quick!" said Meg.

"I'm all undressed," said David. It would take him two minutes too long to retie his necktie. He looked at Meg. "But you're not! Besides, he moves better with you on him. You're lighter than I am. He's going to have to float around that ring if we're going to beat Rocket Rhythm!"

It was true. Meg was dressed and ready for center stage. She had been so busy watching the show, she had even forgotten to take off her gloves.

"*You* rode well in the hack class, *you* can ride him now!"

Meg snapped the helmet strap under her chin. The judge was waiting, and Rocket was already walking around the ring. David gave her a boost and helped shorten the stirrups. In a few steps, they were walking behind the chestnut champion. Meg felt the eyes of the judge and the audience sizing her up next to Mary Keith. David was right; Blue moved a bit more brightly with Meg's lighter weight on his back.

"They look very nice, don't they?" remarked Father.

The children showed their ponies at a walk, trot, and canter. Meg pretended she was calm and experienced, that she had done all this before. It was hard to imagine showing in Short Stirrup after a thrill like this! Then she remembered Lady Jane, all alone down in her stall. She worried: What if Janie was trying to lie down again? She wanted to leave the ring, forget the stupid championship, and go to her pony, who needed her!

But Meg had a job to do for David *and* for Blue, who had been such a good pony today and who did his best for both of them. The announcer asked the two girls to line up in the center of the ring.

Meg listened to the name being announced as if it belonged to someone else:

"PONY CHAMPION, DIXIE BLUE DEVIL—"

The little blonde girl handed her a silver bowl, and she heard her name:

"RIDDEN BY MEG JACKSON."

Mary smiled and said, "Nice going, Meg." The girl presented Mary with a red-and-white reserve place ribbon.

Meg and Blue were surrounded by proud parents and admiring friends. David hugged his pony happily, relieved that it was over. Deep inside, he realized that it did not take a championship ribbon to prove his pony was the greatest in the universe. He was much more than a winner; he was an important member of the family.

For Meg, the moment was pure magic. It was almost like make-believe, but the ribbon in her hand was real enough and very beautiful. She couldn't wait to show it to her friends at school.

Back at the stable, Meg need not have worried about Lady Jane, for at that very moment she was being tenderly cared for by her younger brother and her cousin. Tommy was carefully grooming her, while Anna was cleaning her stall. Lady Jane's eyes were half closed. She seemed to enjoy all the attention.

Meg felt a pang of jealousy when she saw them, but then she remembered how much she'd loved brushing Lady Jane when she was little. Anyway, it was good to have some help when you had more than one pony to take care of.

"Would you mind giving me a hand here?" said David. Meg held Blue while David took off his tack and put it away. It felt so good to be inside the cool, breezy stable. Blue was glad to have a rest.

"Meg, can I give Janie this carrot?" asked Anna, her big eyes looking earnestly up at her cousin.

"No! Not today, Anna. She was really sick last night," said Meg. And for once, Janie was not even interested. Still, Meg knew Anna was disappointed.

Across the aisle, Another stuck his head out of his window as far as he could reach. He hoped someone would see him. Anna went over to pat him. He nodded his head and opened his jaws in an enormous yawn.

The children laughed and laughed.

"Another," said Anna, "don't you know you should cover your mouth!"

"Well, you'll have to forgive him," said Mother. "He had a very hard night last night."

"Hey, Anna. I'll bet Another would love a carrot. He sure isn't sick!" said Tommy.

Anna held the carrot by its end so she could reach the big horse. Another took it and devoured it greedily in two bites and shook his head, looking for more.

"Another, you're nothing but a big pony dressed up in horse's clothing!" said Mother.

"You aren't a pony, but I'll tell you something: you're still a champion as far as Lady Jane and I are concerned," said Meg as she reached over to give him a kiss. "If it hadn't been for you, who knows what would have happened to Janie!"

Meg helped David sponge off Blue and put him in his stall. Then she and Anna checked once more to see that Janie was all right.

"When can we ride her?" asked the little girl.

"Soon. Tomorrow, maybe. But first we have to take *very* good care of her." Meg could tell Anna had been hoping to have a ride today, and she tried to think of something to make her cousin feel better.

"I'll bet you would do well riding Lady Jane in a show. She is just your size!"

Anna beamed. To show a fine pony like Lady Jane would be a special treat.

"Maybe you could ride her in our next horse show when she gets better. Did I ever tell you about the time she won the Short Stirrup championship? She was so great. I was just a little older than you are, and it was my first championship—" Meg walked out of the stable with her arm around Anna, who listened carefully to every word she said.

Father stood waiting, ready to go home. Everyone was happy to leave the stable behind. It had been a long, busy day. The children laughed when he called, teasing, "The only passengers allowed in this car are the Pony Champions and their crew! Let's hit the road!"

Acknowledgements

I wish to thank the following individuals for their help and cooperation in making the photographic illustrations possible: Elizabeth, Gordon, and Taylor Sutton; Cynthia Carroll; Mark Foley, D.V.M.; Mr. and Mrs. Thomas B. Bishop and Marianna Bishop; W. Patrick Butterfield; Anna McKnight; Samantha, Sharon, and Zachary Predmore; Kathy, Meredith, and Drew Kelly; Cara Llewellyn; Shorey, Lois, and Daniel Myers; and the owners and managers of The Farm, Millington Stable, and Riverdale Farm.